Books by Robert Coles

CHILDREN OF CRISIS
*A Study of
Courage and Fear*

DEAD END SCHOOL

DEAD
END
SCHOOL

DEAD

END

SCHOOL

by ROBERT COLES

Illustrated by Norman Rockwell

An Atlantic Monthly Press Book
Little, Brown and Company

Boston   Toronto

ATLANTIC–LITTLE, BROWN BOOKS
ARE PUBLISHED BY
LITTLE, BROWN AND COMPANY
IN ASSOCIATION WITH
THE ATLANTIC MONTHLY PRESS

Published simultaneously in Canada
by Little, Brown & Company (Canada) Limited

PRINTED IN THE UNITED STATES OF AMERICA

To Bobby and Danny
and to their mother

DEAD

END

SCHOOL

1

MY NAME is James, same as my father's. My mother calls me Jimmy. My father was Jim and I can't forget how it was when he was around. It was better — he was there, big and always pushing at us to get up and start the day. And he called me Jim.

My father worked as a plumber's helper, and he took care of buildings for extra money. It meant he was practically never home, except to eat and sleep, and maybe late in the evenings and on Sundays, when we went to church. But my mother was always saying how lucky we were, to have the dollars coming in and good food and bikes and everything. She used to say that if things kept going the way they were, we could move out of the city and find a place of our own.

But it never happened. Instead one day last winter a boiler Dad was working on exploded or something. He was rushed to the hospital and that was the end. My mother talks about him, usually when she wants us to do something for her, or study.

"Your father took care of us, and what would he think if he saw you loafing around, doing nothing and expecting to be waited on, hand and foot? If you're going to be lazy you'll get nowhere. Your father never wasted a minute. He finished school, and he worked himself into a trade. He read books and kept himself up on the world. He spoke good English and his bosses told him he was one of the smartest men around. And he was dependable, which is not like some of his children."

I can't answer her when she gets going like that.

The only thing to do is clench your teeth and move your toes, or pinch yourself, or something. There are seven of us, so we take our turns listening and she never keeps it up for long. I'm the next to oldest and I get it the worst. She ends by telling us that we do better than a lot of people, and we have to keep it that way.

That's my mother's biggest idea, to keep us moving ahead. Even when we slide back, she says, we can turn it into something good. When she had to go on welfare, she said the regular checks would give her time to help us read and study. The only trouble was the checks weren't big enough, and something had to happen or we'd be thrown on the street for not paying the bills. So, that summer we decided to move.

Mary, my older sister, said: "You watch. Ma will tell us to be glad, and that it's about time we moved."

Well, Ma said it, almost exactly. We hated to leave, but she kept on saying it would be the best thing in the world. We would be near Grandma, who could take care of us, while Ma got some work on the side. We'd have more money, and eat better. And we'd be switching to a new school, so that might be a real improvement.

"You wait and see," she said the day the movers came. "You'll go over to that Saunders School and like it fine, a whole lot more than you've ever liked school before."

I asked why, and she said she just knew. My brother Billy said that we could be on a sinking ship with no one around to save us, and Ma would be telling us how lucky we were — we'd learn all about the ocean, and what it was like at the bottom, the fish and shells and all that.

Anyway, we moved.

"Are you kidding?" I said to my mother when I saw the new place. It has four rooms. As you walk through, each room is smaller than the last until you get to the kitchen and can barely breathe.

She exploded. "Am I kidding? You'll see about how I'm kidding if you don't shut your mouth and get down to work unpacking. I'm tired of you and your lazy-rich ideas. This place is our home from now on, and when I'm through it *will* be a home. We'll make it one by sweat, not complaining. Do you hear?"

I heard. She made so much noise it was hard *not* to hear. She had each one of us doing something, except my two little brothers and they're babies.

The apartment was a dirty mess. But Mary and I helped clean it. We got the curtains up, and some pictures my mother cut out of magazines a long time ago, one of some grass and a river, and one of a man with a dog going hunting someplace. We moved the furniture all around, too, and finally we settled for good where to keep it.

There were some holes in the wall, and my mother got boards and made me nail them up. She wasn't going to take any chances with rats.

It took three days to fix up that kitchen. My mother wouldn't even cook in it to begin with. The stove didn't work, and it was filthy dirty. The refrigerator made funny noises and shook the floor when it cut off and on. The lights were burned out. Grandma brought over food or we went across the street and ate in her house. We had chicken and french fries and all the ketchup we wanted. That's the difference between Grandma and Ma. Grandma fries everything, real crisp, and then lets you eat as much as you want, and use all the ketchup you want. But Ma says "no" all the time about ketchup, and she says fried food isn't good for you. When we tell her that Grandma has lived longer than anyone else, no matter what she eats, then Ma pretends not to hear.

In a couple of days we were settled. I missed the old place, but we had the same beds and chairs and everything. The big trouble was that almost all of us had to sleep in one room, my three brothers and me, and my older sister Mary, too. She was really mad, getting stuck with us. My mother sleeps in the other bedroom with the two babies. Mary keeps threatening to move out and sleep in the kitchen, and we tell her to go ahead, but she doesn't. I don't know why she's complaining. My three brothers are all younger than me, and we all have to sleep in one big bed. Mary has her own bed.

It was August, and hot as blazes. The new place was awful. Even though it was cooler on the street, I felt funny about being there. I tried making friends, but no luck. All I found was little kids. I asked one of them where everyone was.

"They're in the gas station talking, or the clubs playing pool. Or they hide out someplace."

So I went to a drugstore and the man told me to get out. I saw an empty store and could hear voices and they didn't sound grown-up. I was scared but I put my hands in my pockets and tried to look real cool. The door was open, and I kicked it wider open and walked in. There were about ten guys there,

[9]

mostly standing around, and a few sitting playing cards.

"Hey, mister, what do you want?"

"I'm new here. We just moved in, and I'm trying to find something to do."

"Well look somewhere else. Hear?"

"You mean . . ."

"Yeah, we mean *get out* — and *fast.*"

I must have waited a second, and he started moving toward me. The next thing I was in the street, running.

I tried a few other places, and there'd be a few guys my age, but they let me know right away that they didn't like strangers.

It got so I almost liked being upstairs. I did a lot of odd jobs around the house because they were *something* to do. My mother and I, we did a lot of talking about my dad, and why we moved, and what it was going to be like later, when maybe we'd have more money, and I would be older, and in college, she said.

And there was always my grandma around, talking about God and telling one story after another.

My grandma calls herself a "lay preacher," and she sure works herself up reading the Bible and going to the tabernacle. She won't even call it church. She says it's a "tabernacle" we go to. Every time we ask her why, she tells us the same thing: "In the Bible it says that people moved all over, from place to place, never making a real home. They used to pray in tabernacles, tents. They would set them down in the desert, and ask God to make it easier for them, and then they would pick themselves up and keep going. That's how it is for us, Jimmy, even now, and that's why we have to stay and pray longer than other people. And that's why we go to a tabernacle and not a church."

2

FROM the middle of August, when we moved, to when we started getting ready to go back to school was the longest, slowest time I've ever put in.

When the first day of school finally came, I woke up glad to be going — gladder than ever before, I'll tell you. I forgot about everything, the moving and Dad and how hot it was in the apartment. I kept on thinking there would be a lot of guys there at school, and it might be a real good place, like my mother said, and I could make some friends. So I got dressed fast and sang away at breakfast. Mary said I was singing a little off the track, but I didn't mind.

My mother made pancakes for me, my favorite of everything, and told me to drown them with syrup if I wanted. Grandma came over, and helped cook. So we had everything on time and none of us could complain. Grandma said one of her long, preachy prayers, with her hands up in the air, like she does every year when we start school. My mother was making sure we got dressed right, Mary and Billy and me, so we'd look good to the teachers, and my grandmother was saying a prayer for each of us.

She walked over to Mary and told her she was going to be the best girl in school, and everyone was going to like her. Then she added, "Please God." And she told Billy and me she wanted us to be good like our dad was.

Meanwhile Ma kept saying "yes" to what Grandma told us, but she was more interested in seeing that we were all "new and shiny"—that's what she said. I was afraid it was putting on too much, the new shirt and the bow tie, but I didn't say anything. I thought to myself I could always unclip the tie and put it in my pocket.

It was then, after I said goodbye and was on my way to school, that I met Larry. I was thinking I'd soon be near the corner, and the next thing was to take a right. I turned the corner, and there he was.

"Hey, boy, where you going?" he said softly.

I wasn't sure he meant me, so I looked around, and nobody else was there.

"I mean you. You going to school?"

"Yes. And you?"

"I guess. My old lady just gave me the bounce. She slammed the door and said if I didn't show up at school, I'd better not come home."

"Did she mean it?"

"Are you kidding? Her? That's a laugh."

I didn't say anything. I just kept walking. And then he grabbed me by the arm.

"You going to Saunders?"

"Yes."

"You're headed the long way around, man."

"I thought this was the best way to get there."

"If you want to waste half your life getting there, it is. You want to play games with every traffic light around, and let the cops tell you where to cross?"

"How do *you* go?"

"Well, I'll tell you. It's a big secret, but I'll let you in on it — if you can keep your mouth shut."

He still held on to my arm and I was doing like he said. I kept quiet. He pointed to an alley between two buildings, and I had to follow him.

What a shortcut! When he let go of me I didn't know what to do — there was so much glass and garbage and stuff that I stopped trying to dodge it after a while. Besides, he gave me a look when he saw what I was doing, trying to step over things, or around them. He didn't say anything, and I didn't. It seemed like making no noise was part of going through the alley.

Every minute or so he stopped to look at something; an old shoe, or a cereal box, or some cards. One of them was an ace of diamonds, and he showed it to me, and then put it in his pocket. He kicked a loose piece of wood in one fence. Then he showed me how the bricks in a building were loose, so you could pull them out. I almost tripped over a tire, and just as I thought I was getting used to the backyards and everything, I saw some rats eating garbage and they didn't even turn when we walked by.

I felt bad in my stomach. I thought I was going to throw up the whole breakfast I just ate. I tried not to show him how I felt. I remember that I kept walking. I concentrated on my feet, on keeping them going one after the other. And from the corner of my eye I could see the rats, fat, brown, bigger than cats. They stood still, looking, and then moved a little, and their tails followed, and they made noises.

I was glad when we left the alley to cut through the hall of a building. I felt much better being inside again.

"It's only a couple of minutes after the next yard. We go through a back street and it leads us almost right to the school. It's much faster this way, and there's no one bothering you."

"Do you go this way every day?"

"Mostly. I know another shortcut, but it's longer.

I like to go any way that gets me away from the lights. They're stupid. No cars are coming, but the light is green and you're supposed to wait. Then a pile of cars show up, and it's red, so they sit and burn up gas, even if there's no one around to want to walk across. Stupid. Things are done stupid, and all they do in school is give you more stupid rules."

And then we were on the street. Just to the right of us was the school, like I saw it a week before with my mother. Only there were people all around, and I was glad I had a friend. I must have smiled at him or something, because he grinned.

"I'm Larry. What's your name?"

"Jim."

"O.K., Jim. You want to try the alley again going home?"

"Sure."

"What grade you in?"

"Sixth."

"Think you'll ever finish it?"

"I hope so."

"I'm starting sixth, too, and it's going to be a waste of time, the biggest waste anyone ever dreamed up. Just wait."

Like before, I didn't know what to say back, but we were practically inside the building, so I just said something about having to go to the office to find out what to do.

"You'll be there all day, kid. But who knows, we may collide in the cafeteria. If you want to stand right outside the door we came in, I'll pick you up when school's over."

The next thing I knew he was gone. I thought to myself that he might even know a shortcut to his room.

I moved in the direction Larry showed me, but I didn't seem to be getting anywhere. The school was much bigger than I remembered. When Ma and I had walked over to look at it I told her it looked just like the old one, same broken windows and writing all over the walls and everything else. Even the fence around it was coming down. But my mother said no, it's what's inside that counts. "That will be different." Well, it was. The halls were longer, and there were even more kids than before, so many I couldn't see how there was enough air for everyone to breathe.

The corridors went on, and turned corners, and I had to ask someone else about the principal's office. I saw a teacher and asked her.

"End of the hall, last door to the left. And pick up your feet. It's late."

So I did what she said and there was the door with the sign: OFFICE. WALK IN. I turned the knob just as the bells all let go. The corridors were suddenly empty. I waited for a second before pushing the door open. Then I was afraid someone might come down the hall and see me standing there with my hand on the door, so I just swallowed and leaned on the door and the next thing I knew I was inside.

3

IT WAS the biggest office I ever saw, almost like a hall or something, and there were three women in it. They didn't even look up when I came in, and I stood there, not knowing what to say or do. I thought to myself I could be a holdup man and they wouldn't know it, or I could grab some pencils and paper and a lamp on the desk near the door and just walk out, and it wouldn't make any difference to them.

I kept on swallowing and getting ready to cough or something to make them look up and see me. But then one woman dropped a pencil and couldn't reach it from her chair, so she got up to look for it, and that's how she noticed me.

"The principal is a very busy man," the secretary told me first thing.

I told her my name and that I was transferring from the Lawrence Simpson School.

"You'll have to wait your turn," she said, and went back to finding that pencil.

It was O.K. at first, just sitting there on a stool and hearing her talk on the phone. She was always either apologizing or getting angry. Once she turned to me and told me there were twice as many children in the building as there ought to be. I didn't say anything. I didn't know if I was supposed to or not.

I just sat there watching and listening. Someone would call and she would say she was sorry, that she would be "right on it." She was always being sorry. Then on one call she really let go: "I'm not here to give messages. We're very busy here. I'm doing the work of five already." She took the message, but I don't know when it was delivered.

I never saw her smile once. She had a crazy habit of taking her glasses off, rubbing her eyes, then putting her glasses on again and moving them up and down her nose, as though she wanted to give them some exercise. She had a run in her stocking. I didn't like her keeping me so long, but I also began to feel sorry for her. I didn't have anything else to do, so I kept looking at her and then the ceiling and then the windows — boy, were they dirty — and then back to her again.

Nothing happened all morning. The stool got harder and harder, but I didn't dare say anything. I wanted to get up and walk around the office; but no, I had to sit there. Then the secretary took a big candy bar out of her desk and nibbled on it. She looked up suddenly and offered me a piece. "I'm too fat anyway," she said. But I didn't dare take it and she finished it.

Finally I heard the clock strike noon. Then the lunch bell rang and the office was full of the noise of kids walking and talking in the corridors. I stood up and walked toward the secretary. She seemed surprised, as if she thought I had left a long time ago. She had a fast mind, though. In a second she had her advice for me: "Why don't you go have lunch and then come back. Your records may be here by then, and maybe we'll know what room to put you in."

After she pointed the way to the cafeteria I was on my own. I've never seen so many boys and girls in all my life. I kept hoping I would bump into Larry. The noise in the halls and in the cafeteria was so loud that I wanted to run, or scream louder than the sound of the noise, or do something to get it out of my ears.

I stood in a line that went all around the back of the cafeteria. The lunches were supposed to be free for me my mother had told me, but I began to wish I had brought a jelly sandwich with me. I was sure they would run out of food. After a long time I got to the counter. A lady scooped some soup into a bowl and put it on my tray. Then another one gave me some spaghetti and nodded me on to the milk tray. I took a glass and was through with the line. I stood there wondering where to sit and smelling sour spaghetti sauce and wishing I was back home. A teacher came over and told me to stop dreaming and sit down.

"There's only five minutes left to lunch period," and she pointed to an empty chair.

The table was crowded with elbows and dishes. I ate fast and kept looking for Larry. Nobody talked to me and I pretended very hard that I was expecting a friend. Suddenly the bell rang and everyone headed for the door. I went back to the office.

The secretary was gone, but another lady was there. She at least smiled when she told me to sit down. I did, wondering if I would be there the rest of the day and go home without knowing which room and teacher were mine. The secretary came back and she looked bothered when she saw me. She said the principal would take care of my problem soon. "Soon" turned out to be after another hour. Several times I got a look from her telling me she wished I'd disappear, but finally she called out my name as if she didn't know where I was, and she took me into the principal's office.

I got scared going in, so scared that I don't remember even now what the place looked like. I do remember that the principal was bald and he was talking to a machine, but it wasn't a telephone. He didn't say a word to me. He wrote something on a piece of paper and handed it to the secretary. In seconds we were out of the office and I was on my way up to Room 18, dragging my feet, and with only an hour of school left.

The secretary opened the door, pushed me inside and closed the door behind me. I stood there feeling stupid. Then I heard Larry's voice. "Jim, you made it." I was surprised and scared — that he was there and he was so friendly and he dared shout like that.

Then I began to notice the room. The teacher was out. That was why Larry spoke as if we were in the alley again. The classroom was cold. The radiators were there, lining the wall, and they were covered with rust and dirt. My room at home may not be the best place, but at least it has curtains, and the ceilings and walls aren't so cracked. When the teacher came back she told me to sit in the back of the room and keep quiet.

That was a joke, telling me to keep quiet. No one else was quiet. No one

seemed to pay any attention to her. She banged a pointer on her desk and a few boys sat down and everyone talked softer, but that was all. Larry motioned to me to sit on his side of the room, and I did — on a stool against the back wall.

There was a whole bunch of us there on stools just like the one in the office. There weren't enough desks to go around. A girl told me I'd have to learn to use a book to write on.

I sat there for a few minutes, sort of taking in the room and figuring out what was going on. With each tick of the clock I was more disappointed. I felt like walking out and going home. Then Larry reached back and poked me.

"We can have fun here, Jim. She won't pay us much attention back here, so don't worry yourself over her."

"What if she catches you talking?"

"She just screams 'shut up.' Then she eats another Lifesaver. Then she screams again. She makes more noise than anyone else. Sometimes she cries, but that doesn't happen often. She's pretty tough, she's been here a long time, and they say she's waiting to retire. She likes pushing us in and out of the room and banging that pointer on her desk."

Suddenly the teacher showed us she wasn't only counting the minutes until the bell rang. She banged the pointer harder than usual, and then left it on her desk and came right up to Larry.

"You are a little troublemaker, and it won't be long before you'll be leading a gang. I'm tired of your behavior and I'm giving you one last warning today. If you don't keep your mouth shut I'll have you removed from this classroom, and I'll refuse to let you back in."

Larry didn't say a word. For the first time since I came into the room there was real quiet. It felt funny, like someone had fired a shot. Everyone was so busy trying to find out what had happened that they stopped talking. It lasted, too. We all sat quiet for about a half an hour. The teacher passed out books, four of them to each of us. Three were so old they were falling apart, but one was new, and I was the first to sign my name in it. *World Geography for Beginners* it was called, and there were plenty of maps, and pictures of people in Africa and Asia, mostly sitting around or working on farms. She told us to read Chapter One and get ready for a quiz tomorrow. Then the bell rang, and that ended the quiet, and school. No one waited to be dismissed. The whole room got up and moved so fast that the door was jammed full, and I was alone in the back.

Larry waited for me.

"You're slow, Jim, you're slow. You don't walk out of here, you run — fast."

"Why? Look what happens. The door gets packed and you have to wait anyway."

"That's the trick, to get out before it happens."

Pretty soon we were away from the building heading for the alley. Larry couldn't get school out of his mind, though.

"That teacher, she thinks she can scare me, but she can't, and she knows it. She's so scared I'll get even with her, she drives away from here doing a hundred an hour. They come in here, those lousy white teachers, from clear across town and think they're kidding us, telling us they want to make us learn. All they want is their money. They don't care about us, they hate us. I know that just by looking at them."

"You don't mean that!"

"I do. She wanted to kill me when she came toward me, but she didn't dare. She's a coward. She just stood there and didn't do a thing. Did you see?" He was boiling over. "A lot of talk. She was scared. She kept opening and closing her fist, as if she wanted to belt me but didn't dare. I hoped she would — I wanted her to, I did. Then I'd have murdered her."

He couldn't stop talking. He kept going, faster and faster.

"I would wait for her to move in on me, then trip her — and the big fat thing would go down. Then I'd get a stranglehold on her, and let her scream. Then I'd squeeze." He was jumping up and down, and I was scared — but I couldn't stop listening.

"What if the principal came?"

"We could take care of him, too. He's an old man, and just as scared as she is. No one would dare help them, anyway. The teachers are scared. And the kids are on our side. It would be easy. We'd take over."

"They'd have the cops over here."

"The cops? The cops don't want trouble with us. I've slashed a few tires on the teachers' cars, and they don't even report it. Even if they did, the cops would laugh at them. The cops, they just want no pain. They'd tell the teachers to go take care of themselves, like the cops have to. The trouble with you, Jim, is you don't know what's going on in the world."

"Why do you go to school at all?"

"I go because I'm waiting for the right thing to come along, then I'll stop so fast no one will be able to trace me. The way I see it, you go to school until you locate yourself. Then you leave."

It was getting late and I knew my mother was worrying because I wasn't home right after school. I tried to hurry us both up by saying I had errands to do. Larry was too smart, though.

"I know. Your mother wants you. That's nice! My mother wouldn't miss me if I never showed up again — and am I glad. She's got nine of us, the old lady, and sometimes she messes up and forgets whose name is whose. Once I told her to fix her memory straight, and she hit me harder than for anything I'd ever done."

I kept quiet, because I figured Larry just wanted to get something off his chest. He must have been expecting me to say something, but there wasn't anything to say. I wished I were somewhere else.

[33]

And then he changed.

"Come on. We can make better time through the alley. I'll race you."

So we raced, and I ran faster than ever before in my life.

He was faster, though. And he has a longer wind to him. But he stopped first, and only a few inches ahead. He was as sweaty as I was, and he looked as if he'd been fighting, or come out of a jungle, or something. We'd raced right though the entire alley, and neither of us had any breath. Finally, I said "So long" to Larry. He said he'd see me tomorrow and disappeared around the corner.

4

THE NEXT day I left the house early, and I thought I'd stop near Larry's house and wait until he came out. But he was already there, sitting on the steps. I told him I was sorry to be late.

"You're not late, so don't be sorry." We started walking, and I didn't say anything, because he seemed angry. We walked through the alley, and once or twice Larry threw a rock at a window, or kicked a can or a piece of wood. Just as we came near the street he suddenly turned around and went back on his tracks a few steps and stepped on an eggshell.

He made sure it was smashed and then he turned to me and said, "I hate the morning."

I said it was all the same to me, morning or afternoon.

"I like the evening. There's more going on. And it's the only time I get any food out of my old lady and my big, bossy sister. They say I can eat in school, and I don't need breakfast. They're right. Why eat a lot of food to have energy in school? I don't need breakfast because I've been doing nothing but sleeping. Besides, the only time we have anything is when the Welfare check comes. Then we have coffee cake, if I can beat my sister to it before it's all gone. It's *my* idea that breakfast is a waste. They say they'd give me eggs and sausages every morning if I did better in school. What a joke."

"Did you try?"

"No. Why should I? I knew they were bluffing. They don't have a cent to buy breakfast for me, or anyone else. My mother, she screams at us to obey her, and go to school, but what she really wants is us out of her way. If I went up to the moon with the astronauts, she'd be so glad you wouldn't believe it, because I'd really be no trouble then."

"I know. My mother always tries to get me to mind her, too."

"Does she beat you up?"

"Well, no, not very hard."

"Man, you are a lucky guy on this street. My old lady hits me so much I figure she just has to do it, to let off steam. I don't pay attention anymore, I just say to myself: Larry, you've got to take it from her until you can get out and set up your own place. So don't feel too bad for yourself, and keep your eyes open. Someday you'll find a deal."

Neither of us said anything more till we came to the school, and then Larry laughed. "Well, if it isn't the old school building, still standing, crutches and all. You can hear her getting ready to die. She can't breathe, and her head is splitting but she's got no aspirins. One of these days we'll come here and we'll think we've got lost or something, because the building won't be here. Then we'll take a closer look, and and we'll see a big pile of bricks and dust. It'll mean the building finally fell down — there it'll be, all sprawled on the ground, knocked out, like it should have been maybe one hundred years ago. There isn't anything good that's happened there for at least that long."

That day we did exactly nothing. The teacher, Miss Turner, came in with a cold, or something. She kept on excusing herself to go cough and sneeze. She used up a whole package of Kleenex, and she sent one girl for water every ten minutes or so.

After an hour or so we had recess, and we didn't know what to do. Larry said they're supposed to let us talk, and if the weather is good we should go out in the yard, but they're scared.

"She tells us to get up and stand near our desks for five minutes and keep quiet. So we talk, but we can't really talk like we could if she wasn't around. She's afraid to tell us we can really relax, so the recess is a big joke. And they never let you out in the yard. They know we'd all leave."

After recess we just sat around and read. She told us to get ready for lunch by doing some reading in our history book, and then we'd be asked questions later, in the afternoon. So I sat there, looking at a picture of Benjamin Franklin, and reading a few pages on him and Philadelphia until finally the bell rang and we could leave that room and get some food. I noticed the teacher was out of her chair before we were, even Larry. She just walked out and left the room to us, but we didn't want it any more than she did. We followed her fast.

After lunch Miss Turner made someone get up and read about Benjamin Franklin and he made all kinds of mistakes but she didn't seem to care. Only when he paused, or stopped, did she look up. Twice she said "Keep going." I couldn't stop myself from turning toward Larry and saying that she just wanted him to read all day, like a machine or something, to keep some noise going in the room. Finally he came to the end of the section, and he told her so. She said "Oh," and asked someone else to go on. She didn't seem interested, so why should we be, I thought.

The reading went on and on. I was watching the clock. The hand had just turned another minute, the twelfth I counted, when the principal walked in. He came to the back of the room. I leaned hard over my book because I knew he was right behind me. Then he walked slowly to the front and the teacher smiled and the reading stopped. Larry gave me a wink and a sneer and slouched down in his seat.

"Your teacher will hand out to each of you a letter you must take home and have your parents sign. One parent will be enough. Some of you may have observed that the school is a bit crowded. We are sorry to say that the Fire Department has told us that we simply cannot keep the present number of children

in this building. We've been much over the number we're equipped to handle for years, but this year it's really become too much. The Fire Inspector was here yesterday to tell us we had to do something, and immediately. As a result I have conferred with the superintendent of schools and other officials, and we are going to move a number of you to another school, not too far away. This class will go to the Francis Bacon School, and a fifth grade class will go to the John Quincy Adams School. We don't have time to figure out the distance from each child's home to new schools — it's an emergency, and we have to act right now. So you go home and read the letter over with your parents. It'll tell you all you need to know. Tomorrow you come back here — with the letters signed, as I said — and we'll arrange for your transfer. It should only take an hour or so, and you'll be on your way to your new school."

He wanted to know if there were any questions.

Who knew what to ask? For one thing, the bell rang in the middle of his speech. And besides, what could you say? I did find myself wondering what my mother would ask *me* — but I figured the letter would explain everything. Anyway, he didn't really wait for us to think and say anything. In the time it would have taken me to raise my hand he was out of the room — and we were at the door after him.

"Do you think it'll be like this at the Bacon School, Larry? Where is it, anyway?"

"You don't know? It's a couple of blocks down from here. It's much smaller than this, and even older."

"It can't be older."

"Jim, you're a real nice guy. You actually trust people, and you think things will get better if you just pray or something. You're stupid."

"Maybe *you're* the one who's stupid. All you can see is how bad everything is. I don't agree with everything my mother says, but I sure don't see why you want to knock down everything automaticlike, before you even get a look at it."

"Come off it, Jim. I know you're a real good boy, and you believe what you're told. But you're fooling yourself. The principal came and told us there are too many of us. So he's getting rid of us. That man doesn't really care what happens to us."

"You don't know what you're talking about. He could have promised to build a bran'-new school for us, and you would have smelled a rat somewhere."

"When he does something like that, there *will* be a rat to smell."

"Larry, you'll get fooled one of these days."

"And you'll be looking for the best and you'll get it, like it'll fall down from the sky."

We went home by another shortcut — through a building and then a yard behind three stores. He showed me where he used to take a can of food or a loaf of bread. Once he was caught, and if he was caught again it would be the police.

When we came to his house, I told him I'd see him tomorrow and was on my way. He shouted after me, "Jim, the way we just came, that's part of a shortcut to the Bacon School. I thought I'd break you in fast."

That's Larry, a step ahead of everyone!

5

WHEN I got home I handed the letter to my mother. She read it, real fast, her head going back and forth. She read parts of it out loud, which she does when she gets excited. ". . . your child has been chosen as one of a group of students to be transferred to the Francis Bacon School. We are presently so overcrowded that we are obliged to make this transfer for the health and safety of our children. I am confident that the Francis Bacon School will offer them the same high standards of education . . . Will you please sign your name below and have your child return this letter to us. We will then make the

[46]

transfer as planned. Sincerely yours. C. A. Jones, Principal."

"Who does Mr. C. A. Jones think he is? Who gave this to you?"

"The principal. He came up himself and told us about it."

"What did the other children say?"

"Nothing. It doesn't make any difference — does it? Larry didn't care, and I could see no one else did, either. They just wanted to get out of school and go home. I heard one girl say her mother wouldn't like it, but *she* liked it, because it would mean a few days of being mixed up, and not having to work, until we got settled again."

"I don't care what Larry says. I can tell what he's like already. What's the name of that girl? I'd like to talk with her mother."

"I don't know."

"Why is it you only know Larry's name? Keep it up — and you'll become like him, a troublemaker."

[47]

Then she went into the kitchen, and turned off the stove, so she could go across the street to see Grandma. I could tell she was upset, just like I thought she'd be. But she was even more upset than that. She started banging the dishes and she kicked the door. She muttered something to herself, and then I heard her mention my father. I think she said something like "What would his father do?" She took off her apron and threw it on the floor. Then she started looking for the letter, which she must have put someplace in the kitchen, but forgotten where.

"Where is that letter, that letter you brought home?"

It was right in front of her nose, on the stove.

"I'm not going to take this lying down. I can tell you that, Jimmy. They're not going to shuffle you around from one lousy, overcrowded school to another, as if you're some garbage and they have to empty one barrel into another one that's already filled up. Come with me."

We went across the street — naturally. Grandma was sewing, mending socks and a shirt of mine.

"They're trying to switch schools on Jimmy. After he's just gone and got settled in one, they want to move him to another. And he won't say it, but he's upset. I can tell. He's so upset he doesn't say *anything* — just that it doesn't make a bit of difference to him, whatever they do. Well, that's not the way I'm going to take this. I'm tired of being pushed around. They can do it to us, Momma, but not our children."

My grandmother didn't even understand what was up. She said we should be calm. "Things have a way of working out." She always said that.

After Ma explained some more, Grandma said, "Jimmy's a strong boy. He can go to the new school, and show them how strong he is, and smart, just like he was going to do in the other one. Then more people will know him, and he'll have more friends. Don't you think?"

"No, I don't."

Suddenly my mother got up. She looked at me, and then she came over and took my hand, and that doesn't happen very often. She said we had to go, because she had some thinking to do.

As we went home she was talking to herself.

"I have to talk with a few other mothers and see if they're thinking as I am."

"What do you mean?"

"I'll let you know when I'm sure myself. I'm going to the market and find some other parents to talk to. I don't suppose you know anyone else by name except that lazy Larry."

She was all wrong on Larry, and I told her so. Just because I like a guy, and he and I get along, doesn't mean she has to turn on him. I gave her the names of three or four kids, including two who lived right near us, Frank and Paul. That showed her.

"O.K., I'll leave you alone about Larry. I'll even go see his mother, and tell her how glad I am you two have become such good friends. I'll talk to every mother in the neighborhood if I have to, because I'm going to do something, anything, to make those people in the schools give us a better deal than we've been getting."

When we got home I had things to do, cleaning up the bedroom and washing the floors. I had to get rid of the garbage, and that takes time when there aren't enough barrels to hold it, and you know you're just laying out a supper for rats unless you find a place to put the stuff so they can't get to it.

Meanwhile my mother disappeared. She had said she'd be home in time for supper. It got later and later. Every time we heard steps we thought it was her, but no. Finally Grandma came with some food she had cooked, and we sat down to eat, without Ma.

We finished and Grandma made us say a prayer for having food to eat and a roof on top of us, leaky or not. We were cleaning up when in Ma came, all excited.

"I've talked with three mothers, and they're mad, too. One of them is walking on the ceiling, she's so mad. We're going to talk with a minister she knows, and maybe have a meeting tomorrow. Meanwhile, we're not going to sign the letters, and not letting you go to any other school. If it's a matter of in one trash heap and out of another, or back into the frying pan from the fire, we'll make them know at least one thing. They can't shove us around and treat us like we're dust to be brushed under the rug. No, sir."

"What will I say to the teacher when she asks me for the slip?"

"Tell her I refused to sign it."

"But what if she says go ahead anyway, with the rest of the class, to the new school?"

"You tell her you're going to stay until your mother gives you permission to go. Tell her you don't know how to get to the new school, and that your mother said it's dangerous going there. They're tearing down some old buildings near that Bacon School, so you just let your teacher know I don't want you going to school where they're using dynamite. Those streets are dangerous, with dust and rocks and timbers falling. If you got curious and started going too near the construction, you'd get hurt for sure."

She said she needed a cup of coffee after a speech like that.

It was time for us to go to bed and she was going out again.

6

MA WAS busy the next few days. I went to
school and everyone pretended things were
normal. The move to the new school came closer and
closer and everyone was edgy. Then one morning
when I woke up things were moving. My mother
and grandmother were talking like they had never
gone to bed at all. The breakfast table was all set,
waiting for us, and Ma had a pencil and paper near
her. She was dressed, ready to go someplace, all excited. The coffee was going, and I saw that her cup
was almost empty. When I came into the kitchen she
looked at me as though I was a star, or something.

"I wondered when you'd stir yourself. We've got a lot to talk about before you go to school. Last night I went to the church, and we had a meeting, the minister and about ten of us. We talked over the whole thing, and we decided that you kids aren't moving to the Bacon School. We're all going to school with you today, and we'll tell the teacher and the principal and anyone else. And we'll have a meeting tonight and try to get all the mothers together and figure out what to do next if they start pushing us and telling us off."

"Ma, I don't know what you're talking about. What do you think you're going to do when the teacher says go, and you say stay. She'll call the cops and tell you to get out, fast."

There my mother was, going on and on about what she was going to do. But what about me? I was the one who'd get in trouble.

I started to look at the clock, and wish it was over, the whole day — and maybe the week. I felt my throat getting tight and dry, the way it does sometimes, and I thought maybe I have a cold, and should stay home. Maybe we should forget everything, and go back to school, and maybe it won't be so bad, after all, the new school, and we won't get into trouble, I mean *I* won't.

When I told my mother I thought I was getting sick, she just gave me one of her looks as if she didn't believe me. So then I just shouted at her.

"Leave me alone. Just leave me alone and let me go to school. Leave me out of it, and don't go messing everything up."

I saw her getting ready to talk me into her side of things, and I got even more scared, and suddenly I thought of going away someplace. I looked at the clock again, and told my mother it was late, too late to talk, even though I knew it wasn't. And I turned and ran out.

Was I glad to see Larry! But he gave me a funny

[56]

look. "You're big stuff, Jim. I hear your old lady is running a show."

I wasn't glad any more. "You've heard?"

"Sure I've heard. Not only that, your sweet old ma came to see mine last night, and that was worth more laughs than anything on TV."

"She didn't tell me. She didn't say a word. What happened?"

We stopped in the middle of an alley and Larry sat down on a garbage can and I leaned against a wall. He picked up a handful of stones and as he talked he threw them, one after the other, at pieces of broken glass, at a stack of screens that were more holes than wire. For a couple of minutes he didn't say anything but I knew something was inside him that he wanted to get out, so I just kept quiet.

"Your mother is a pain. She's a pain, like my mother, only worse. Mine, she's no good, and every-one knows it. Yours, she's so good she doesn't know herself how wrong she is."

He stopped for a second, threw a rock, and looked for a second as if he might hit me. Then he stared ahead again.

"My mother's no good. But she does the best she can. She screams at us from when we get up to when we go to bed. That's how I know it's time to wake up and time to go to sleep — I hear her shouting, telling us we're no good, and we're never going to be. So she hates us, me, because I'm a boy and getting older. She's been saying that for a year now: 'Larry, you're getting to it, near to it. You'll start loafing and bumming and ruining people.' That's my mother.

"Now your mother, she came over and started telling the old lady about you and me and the school and all that jazz. It's something to hear. She was all excited, and she wanted to sit and hold my mother's hand, and talk about our *futures*. What a joke!

"Well, my old lady listened. She was smart enough to keep still, probably for fear that because of the whiskey she'd drunk she couldn't say anything straight. Once I almost hit the roof it was so funny — your mother was all fired up in the middle of something, and my mother broke in to ask for a cigarette. I wish I could show it to you in a movie. There would be your old lady talking about the books we read not being good, and how it'll ruin us later, and we'll never get jobs, and my old lady, she just looked her straight in the eye and said, 'Honey, you got a weed for me?' "

Larry laughed like a crazy man and I felt sick. I didn't know what to say, so I started walking. Finally Larry followed and I asked him, "So you'll be transferred?"

"Sure. And so will you, too."

"Even if the mothers march into the school and refuse to let us go?"

"Do you think the principal cares what your mother wants? That will be the day. Just you wait. He'll have the cops escorting your mother to the jailhouse if she doesn't watch her step."

The next thing we were at the school and my mother was calling my name. There were a lot of other women with her, about a dozen. She was holding a sign on a long stick and the minister stood beside her. How my mother got to school ahead of me, I couldn't figure. She must have got a ride, right after I left.

"Jimmy," she called. I pretended not to hear her, and I walked faster. Anyway, I wanted to be with Larry. So I went right inside, fast.

When we came in the classroom there weren't more than five kids there. Miss Turner looked upset and I was sorry for her. When all of us were jammed in that room, making noise and everything, she never seemed too bothered. But now we were only a few and she looked frightened or sick. She ate one Lifesaver after another.

"What's going on here? Who are those people outside? I was supposed to be through with this class, through in a few minutes this morning. All I had to

do was collect those letters and take you over to the Bacon School. I suppose some just went there without checking in here, and someone told me a few of you are getting ready to give us trouble, by trying to stay here, or skipping school altogether."

We kept quiet. It was the quietest I ever heard the room. Then the principal walked in. He was as shaky as she was, and talking a mile a minute.

"I'm tired of the troublemakers in this school. I thought the children were bad, but now I know where they get it from, their parents. Day in and day out the children disobey our regulations and complain about our food or our books, and now all of a sudden they want to stay — so badly they're making a demonstration out of the simple fact we have to transfer a few boys and girls to another school. Who's behind this, that's what I want to know. Because *someone* is, I know that."

We just sat there. He didn't expect us to say anything. He kept wiping his hand on the side of his coat, and his hand looked clean from where I sat. If my mother had done nothing else, she had gotten under his skin, and I figured that should keep me feeling good for a week. But I didn't feel good. I was scared and I wished Ma were home minding her own business.

That secretary I met when I first came to the school suddenly came running into the room. She could move real fast when she had to. There was a lot of whispering and then the principal asked us for our letters. Larry turned in his, and got a smile. So did the three other kids, and they got smiles. I handed them mine, and the principal saw it wasn't signed.

"Did you show it to your mother and father?"

"My father's dead."

"Well, to your mother?"

"Yes."

"Why didn't she sign it then?"

"She said she didn't want to."

"Why not?"

"I don't know."

"You don't?"

"No."

They were angry. The teacher kept staring at me, the principal did, too. The secretary seemed anxious to get back to her office.

"Well, you're all going to the Bacon School this morning. As principal of this school I'm personally going to take you, right now, and turn you over to your new principal. Let's go."

He moved toward the door, and the teacher motioned for us to follow. We did. No one said a word until we passed the principal's office. Then the secretary said she was going to duck in for a second.

We moved on to the front door. The principal opened it and I got a surprise. There were more mothers, more than I ever thought I'd see together for anything. There were other people, too, maybe ministers, maybe college students, the way the Reverend said might happen. There was television, too!

They were just getting set up on the steps. Larry nudged me and said the guys with notebooks were reporters. He spotted cops, too. They were standing around talking with the reporters.

The principal didn't know what to do. I felt like saying, "Well, Mr. Big Deal, you said you were going to take us over to the Bacon School. Let's go." He looked at us, and then at everyone out there. He whispered something to the teacher, and then I heard her say maybe he should wait, and check with city hall. He said that was a "very good idea," and it had just occurred to him, too. So he closed the door and turned around. He said we should wait right here, inside.

We stood for what seemed like an hour. Larry was moving around and *whistling* — in school, right in front of the teacher! And then I saw my mother. She came inside to talk with one of the girls, Vanessa, whose mother had signed the transfer letter. My mother told her that her mother had changed her mind, and she was outside, along with the others. I wanted to ask if Larry's mother was there, but I knew she wasn't. Besides, I was a little scared of Ma. She was my own mother but she seemed different — acting important and far away.

Still the principal hadn't come back. The teacher left to check on what had happened to him. Vanessa wanted to see her mother. My mother said all right we should all go outside. Later we could all come back inside, to stay, whether the principal liked it or not.

So we went outside, following Ma like sheep or something. Larry walked over near the cops and reporters. He just stood there listening. I could tell how he admired those guys. I mean the cops, too, that he always says are no good and crooked.

I stuck close to my mother. I wanted to learn what was going on. She and the minister and a couple of other mothers were in a huddle as though they were getting ready to march across the school yard and score a touchdown. In a few minutes they broke up, and the minister called over the reporters. He told them we were all going back into the school, because it was our school, and they had no right to move us around from one overcrowded school to another. Then the TV cameras started working, and I was in the pictures, I know I was.

Then the mothers started to line us up. My mother shouted that it was time to move. We marched back toward the door, Larry and I in the rear, so we could watch everything. I was sure the door would be locked, but Larry said no. He had heard the reporters say the principal didn't have the right to lock us out. So we marched into the building. It seemed like a new place where I'd never been. Everyone was quiet. It was weird. The reporters followed us in, and so did the policemen.

We just stood in the hall, looking silly. Then the

minister suggested we sit down, right there in the corridor. He said we were to stay there while a "delegation" went to the principal's office.

My mother went, with two ministers and a couple of other mothers. They didn't have to go very far. As they were going to his office, the principal came to meet them. He had a speech all ready.

"I am asking you all to leave. I have to remind you that you are on school property, and that school is in session. You are making a public nuisance of yourselves, and interfering with the education of our children. I am ordered by the school department to ask you to leave voluntarily. If you don't obey we shall have to call the police."

He finished and just stood there. We just looked at him. Then one of the women, I didn't know her, spoke back to him.

"We're not going to move even one inch. If you want us out, you'll have to carry us. This is our children's school, and all we want is for them to stay here. If you won't let them, you'll have to arrest them and us and all our friends. We're tired of you and the rest pushing us around. Real tired."

Everyone clapped and whistled, except Larry and the reporters and the policemen. They just watched.

The principal looked tired. He said he was leaving because he had more to do than bother with us. Then he did leave, "a little fast and a lot mixed-up" said one of the mothers.

Then the Reverend and my mother and another couple of mothers started talking to one another out loud, with the rest of us listening, including the reporters. I heard my mother say "It's out of the frying pan and into the fire. If your children are going to one more dirty, overcrowded school, then they should stay here, where they've started. If they want to take them to a good school, someplace else, that's another thing."

One of the reporters jumped on that, and he asked my mother what she meant.

"I said what I meant — didn't I?"

"Are you trying to say that you want the school department to move your children out of this neighborhood, across the city where the schools aren't crowded?"

"Yes," she said. But she was surprised by the question, and her own answer. I could tell. She and the Reverend looked at each other, and then they whispered something. The Reverend said we should all go home, and meet in the afternoon in the church gym.

What a pain in the neck all this was turning into — talk and talk and more talk. I was getting fed up — and Larry gave me a look as if to say he was glad I was getting wise. We walked home together. Larry was all excited about missing a day of school.

7

I NEVER saw such careful dressing as there was for that meeting. Ma took an hour to put on her best dress. Grandma was weeping and wringing her hands. "You be careful. You be careful."

"Careful about what?" I asked her.

"Just be careful."

You would think we were in trouble with the police, or something.

When we got to the gym it was packed full, with every seat taken. The Reverend started shouting for us to keep quiet, and in a minute or two he got what he wanted. He started praying, and asking us to pray, and blessing us, and then he got down to business.

"We are here because our children have been taken from a school that they have considered theirs, and told to go elsewhere. Where is elsewhere? Another school as bad, as crowded, as old, as dangerous to their health and safety and education as the one they now attend. So we are here because we have had enough. It is as simple as that: we are tired of being treated like castoffs."

Then he went into a speech about all that had happened, how we tried to stay at the Saunders School, but the principal didn't want us. He went on to tell us the latest news, about the meeting between the school superintendent and the mayor, about how the district attorney had gone before a judge asking that we be stopped from "trespassing" on school property. So now it was against the law for us even to step in the Saunders school yard. The police would be there tomorrow, outside the school, protecting it from us — from Larry and me and my mother and all the rest.

Larry was shaking he was laughing so hard.

Several people got up and started talking at the same time. They weren't laughing. They were angry, and they shouted. But they all wanted to say the same thing — that we shouldn't back down before the mayor and the school people and the police, and that we should go to the school and march up and down in front. All the kids should stay out, until they are allowed into the Saunders School.

One lady won out because her voice was the loudest. "I'm glad these children are here with us. They'll keep us from backing down. They'll keep our knees from trembling, and from running away. Anyone who wants to turn around can just look at these children. If they *still* want to back down then I hope the Lord has mercy on them."

Then Larry got real mad.

"What's she know? Who does she think she is, a sidekick of God's? She can look at me all she wants. You know what I'll tell her — I'll tell her, 'Look lady, you're nuts. You're whistling up the wrong tree, and you're going nowhere, fast, and you'd better wise up, or you'll see where people like you get kicked — right into jail.' "

Larry was so mad it scared me. He just went on louder and louder. "They're all alike, those schools. So I'll go to any school they send me, until I can get me a deal that'll make the teachers drool wishing they had one like it, too."

I shoved my hand over his mouth and he shut up.

One old man was talking so soft it was hard to catch his words. I heard the streetcar going past and the rain falling on the roof. Someone sneezed. It was real quiet. People were paying attention and trying to listen. The man stopped and then a lady stood up, big and fat, and with a loud voice. The more she talked the more her voice boomed across the hall.

She said we should all go home. "They've got the law on us now, so we're finished, as we always are. The law is theirs. The law is white. They own the law, white people. You can't do a thing about what they decide in city hall, or wherever they do their deciding. We're still slaves, and don't you forget it. If you think you can do anything, you're fools."

She sat down hard on her chair, so hard you could hear it creak. Again everybody wanted to say something. Two or three people started to talk at the same time, just like in school when the teacher leaves the room. Then my mother spoke up.

"The law belongs to everybody, to all of us. It's our job to make sure it does."

The lady stood up again and shouted, "What do you mean, everybody?"

"I mean you and me and our kids and everybody," my mother said.

"That's talk, just talk," the lady replied and then she sat down.

Then another lady got up and she agreed with the first lady.

"She's right. They keep on saying that we have rights and the police work for us, and all that. Well, go feed your belly on 'rights.' Go find a place with heat and water and pay for it with rights. Go keep out the big, fat, mean rats with rights, and tell the landlord to keep things fixed with rights. My husband died when he was thirty years old because he couldn't get a doctor and the right food. He was sick and dying, and he wanted to die, because he was out of work and tired of being pushed and kicked and hated. You say he had rights. He should have demanded his rights. Well, I'll tell you something, you can't eat rights, lady."

I thought she was never going to stop.

My mother interrupted her: "Every word you say is God's truth. All I'm saying is that there has to be a beginning somewhere, sometime. That's all. If we ask for our rights now, we're starting something. Maybe we won't get them, but we've got to try. You've either got to try or die, try or die."

Larry had an ugly look in his eyes and his voice scared me. "Where does your mother get off, talking like that? She's telling them if they don't do what she wants, they're as good as dead. She's a liar — a dirty liar."

I couldn't say anything. All of a sudden I was hot and sick to my stomach. I felt like throwing up — so I left the room in a hurry.

Larry caught me near the door. He was mad. I couldn't understand him. He was getting madder with each second, and I didn't know why but so was I. I would have hit him but the minister was watching. So I walked away and pretended not to see him.

And then I heard my grandmother's voice. My grandmother — of all people — stood up and said everyone should pray. "I mean *really* pray, when I say pray. When I pray, I pray hard. I sweat at praying. Then I go and try to answer my prayers as best I can, hoping the Lord will show me how."

"Let's not pray, let's go," a woman said. "Where?" a lady next to her said. "Across town" someone shouted from the other side of the hall. "Where across town?" I heard several people ask. "To the good schools, in the good sections," my mother said. A lot of mothers nodded that they agreed. Then some mother asked how we kids would all get there. "By bus," a man said, "the way they go anywhere."

"Well, who will get the bus and pay for it?" the same person asked. "Not the city," she added, and then reminded us that they wouldn't pay us to go where they didn't want us. "They want us right where we are."

They kept on asking questions and answering them, first one person, then another. They even came around to asking the kids about what they thought. A couple of girls said almost the same thing, that they liked the idea of going to a new school, different from the same old thing. A boy who sat near me in class got up and said he'd been wasting his time in school ever since he started. He listed all the bad things about school, and while he was doing it I thought to myself how he sounded just like Larry. But at the end he sure wasn't like Larry. He said he wanted to get out of the rut he was in, and get someplace so that later on when he needs a job he'll be able to find one. Then he looked at his mother and sat down, and she kissed him.

Larry made a loud awful burp. "That's it. That's all I can take without vomiting. That kid is saying just what his sweet mummy tells him, and then she pats him and says aren't you nice. Why don't they all shut their fat mouths and go home and stop making themselves look like third-degree morons?"

"Larry, you're nuts, way off and nuts!" I exploded at him.

"*You're* the one who's nuts, Jimmy. You're like the rest of them, a baby. I knew it all the time, but I sure got proof tonight. All they have to do is wink, and you're running after them, trying to be a good little boy. Wait until later, when you're twenty and begging the city for a relief check. Then you'll see what you'll get out of being like that. You're not only nuts, you're stupid."

Then he moved right into the hall and he shouted: "This is stupid. You're talking nuts, because you'll go to jail if you don't do what they tell you. That's what I think, if you want to know."

Then he turned around and ran out, right toward me. He hit me in the chest, then on the side of the face. I grabbed him. And tried to hold him. Then I kicked him back and

hit his shoulder with a right. He started screaming that I was a "lousy fink and a cop lover." He was throwing punches and I was fighting back, but not as good as he. I screamed "cop lover" back at him. He said something rotten and filthy, and kicked me, and so help me I wanted to bite his hand or stick a knife into him I was so mad. I kept screaming "Go, go," and he and I were hitting back and forth.

Then I heard my mother shouting louder than I ever heard her. Two men pulled us apart, and my mother was all over me, and I was crying.

When things quieted down, Larry had disappeared. I went to the door. It was still raining, and he didn't have a sweater or anything except his shirt, and I could see him, wet and angry. I saw him dash across the street and a car almost hit him, I swear it. You could hear the road wearing the tire down, and the brakes, and the horn. The driver stopped, and all the traffic behind him. People on the street stopped, but not Larry. He kept running and I lost sight of him.

8

FOR TWO days I sat around the house. No school for me. Nothing to do and I wasn't about to look for Larry. Then it was the weekend and all. Still there was no one to talk to. Ma was always busy — outside or inside, going to meetings, and talk, talk, talk, but never to me. And then it was the day! There was a school with room for us. There was a bus for us. We were ready.

I woke up that morning with Ma standing over me. It was like Sunday. She was all dressed up and she had my best clothes in her hand. At first I wanted to turn over and go back to sleep, but when I remembered I got excited. I leaped up and started getting ready. I could smell the bacon and eggs and stuff, and I heard my grandmother in the kitchen — cooking and saying one of those prayers to herself.

They were moving all over the place trying to feed us and get everything set so we could all walk to the bus. My sister Mary and even my little brothers and sisters were all coming to see me off. I felt as if I was going into the army or something, like I'd won a contest or a big prize. In the middle of breakfast I even lost my appetite.

Ma told me not to be nervous, and how great it would be going to that great new school, and wait until I saw it, and the bus ride would be fun. The more she talked the more nervous I got. So I was glad when we finally left the house to go for the bus — the entire family with me, including the babies and my grandma.

There were other families like us, dressed up like

it was Easter or something. I kept wondering about the bus, and if it would be there on time.

On the way we passed Larry's house, and the beginning of the shortcut he showed me. I looked for him. I missed him, and missed going through the alley the way we did, throwing things and looking around. I thought I'd rather be doing that again than going to that bus and going way over the other side of the city, just to go to a school.

We got to the corner where we were supposed to be, and the bus wasn't there. Everyone started looking around, and worrying. It was only twenty of eight. So we stood around, and every once in a while I looked back, figuring maybe Larry would show up. Finally the bus came — a big yellow one, with black letters saying SCHOOL BUS. It was huge.

I waited a while to get on, figuring there'd be plenty of time to sit when the bus was going. Suddenly Larry was there. He was just there, standing with a grin on, talking as though nothing had happened.

"Going somewhere, Jim? A day on the town? Be sure and come back and let us know how those rich cats make out, because we'll be waiting here, our tongues hanging out and our eyes wide, real wide open. So you look for us, and bring it all back."

"Cut it out, Larry. Why not come along, if you're so curious and you want to see what's going on."

"Rich Jim, that's what you'll be. I hear they give you ten dollars when you graduate from that school over there. They pat you on the head, and say how good you are, little black boy, for coming over here, all the way across the city, to be with us and let us know how good we are and how lousy your own people are, your brothers and sisters and friends, everyone you leave to come over here and sit beside us in school and let some of our white rub off on you. The schools around here aren't good enough for you but they are for me."

He turned around and left, almost running.

Then, the driver said "all aboard" and I was the last one on. Ma was crying, so I was glad to get away from her. She was yelling last minute things and wishing me everything she could think up, so I said "O.K., O.K.," and climbed up the steps. The last thing I saw outside was Grandma, telling me the sun was out, and that was a good sign from Heaven. And in a second we were off — right down the street and past Larry, walking to school. He saw me, I know it, but he pretended he didn't. I was looking hard, so I caught him glance up, then he looked away.

Some of us just sat in the bus grinning at one another, at the driver, or out the window, not knowing what to do or say. A few ran up and down in the aisle, even though the driver said not to. We tried out the leather seats, rubbing them with our hands, and we pointed things out — the windows and how to open them, the emergency exit, the pole to lean on if you're standing, or the straps to hold on to. There was seat changing and jostling. A lot of kids wanted to sit up front, near the driver. Others liked the rear of the bus best. There was a long seat there where you could lie down and sleep. One boy said to me we should stake it out, and keep the others away. (In a day or two he changed his mind. He wanted to see how the driver shifted gears and steered.)

In the beginning all we saw were the same buildings we know and live in, one block after another of them. But they looked different. From the bus I could see everything, but not be a part of it. I could see people walking on the sidewalks or sitting on the stairs of the buildings, and I felt away from it all. It was real queer.

When we saw the city hospital, it was really time to pay attention. That building was as far as most of us had ever gone from home. It's just the beginning of getting away. After the hospital came "skid row." (The bus driver called it that.) I never saw so many bars and restaurants before.

A girl in front of me squealed out, "See that guy, he's going to fall right over if he doesn't watch out."

All I could see was the man's face. It was a face asleep or even dead, and it made me feel sick. I saw that look on my father's face only once and I'll never forget it.

Then we went through a section even worse than our neighborhood. I wanted to close the window and hold my breath until we got past those streets. Garbage was everywhere. The buildings were falling down. The street was narrow, and all we could see were broken windows, empty cans and bottles, and some dogs and cats that looked hungry and lost, as if they didn't belong to anyone then, or ever. It was the street my mother used to tell me about. When she got mad she'd try to scare us and tell us if we didn't watch out we'd be *there,* the end of the stop.

"I wish they'd tear it all down — the whole street — so the city would be through with it, too," someone shouted.

"Someday they will," the driver answered back, shouting over the traffic noise. "Maybe in a hundred years, or maybe in a thousand."

"Maybe sooner," I couldn't stop myself from saying. I was glad Larry couldn't hear me.

Next came the big change. We rode through the best part of the city. I never knew there were so many kinds of stores. I saw flowers, books, paper and pencils, furs, hardware, even cards, and each one of them was sold in a different store. The stores we know, the grocery stores, they weren't anywhere to be seen.

"It's all delivery to the rich," the driver said. (He tells us things like that almost every day. He used to work as an janitor in one of the high class buildings we passed by, so he knows.) "They call the stores up and have brought over whatever they want."

"Where do the stores get those flowers, when it's not yet summer?" He knew what to tell me right away: "They have hothouses that grow them — houses all made of glass. Those flowers, they have it better than you and me. Then they bring them into the stores here, and sell them."

"What do people do with them?"

"They put them in the windows, or on their tables."

I saw some in windows, and also some plants growing in boxes outside the windows. You get to see things like that, and those foreign cars and the old furniture that's worth a lot of money.

Then we came to the school. It is right near some big homes and a park that looks so big it could be the whole country. And the school — well, it looked like a school except there were no broken windows. And there was fresh paint. And lights shining through the windows, right in the daylight.

When the bus pulled up I was scared. I heard a boy say we were like guys landing on the moon. We should be cool.

The driver kidded with him: "Why didn't you

bring a flag, so when you land in the school you can plant it there?"

Everyone was pushing to get off the bus. I saw a few girls giggling and one girl tore her dress because she pulled it too hard when she tried to make sure it looked right. When we got on the sidewalk we just stood there for a second. A few boys started to horse around, but they stopped before they could really get going. The bus driver stood on the steps of the bus, looking at the school just as we were doing. Finally he said, "I hate to break up the quiet, but you'd all better go inside."

A few boys and girls were staring at us. One boy came up and said hello. He was *too* nice. A few others just stood and watched us. I didn't know what they thought. Maybe they didn't either. All I knew was that the nearer I came to the door, the slower I walked. All I could hear was my feet. And all I could see was the door. It was painted with a new coat of green, and there wasn't a mark on it.

The building was bright inside and cool even though it was warm outside. I could feel the coolness on my skin. I touched the tile on the walls of the corridor as I walked by. The principal of the school was there, a big tall man with the reddest hair I ever saw. There were two ladies with him — maybe they were his secretaries. They kept on smiling at us, every time we looked at them. The principal broke us up into four sections and then he explained why.

"We want as many of

our children to know you as possible, and so we're sending you to different rooms. I wish you all luck here. We're glad to have you, and I hope you learn all you can here, and like being with us."

Then he motioned us to follow him and the ladies. They led us down the halls, from room to room, leaving a few off at each stop. I was with them to the end, along with four others, and finally we got to our room and he told us to go in and the teacher would be waiting.

When I came inside, I could hardly believe it. There were maps, pictures, and even a large aquarium, the first I ever saw. I wanted to look at the fish, but "stay cool, stay cool" I kept saying to myself. "Don't get too impressed with the coatroom for your jacket and the new books the teacher gave you and having your own desk."

I kept thinking of Larry. He wouldn't show a thing. He'd be so cool he'd get to them. But I kept thinking "it's all mine." I smelled the books, new and clean. I saw the other kids feeling their desks and looking down at the stands of the desks and touching the backs of the chairs. I knew they were as excited as I was, and some were showing it.

It was too good — so good it scared me. I couldn't stop being proud that it was me, Jim, sitting there — for the first time having a desk of my own. Even the others who came with me on the bus seemed different. Their faces had changed and their new clothes finally had a chance to look good. I kept feeling something might go wrong and spoil everything. But nothing did. The white kids just stared, or they smiled when they looked over more than they would if it hadn't been us. I was nervous, and I didn't know what to do. For a while I didn't smile back at the ones who smiled, and then I did. I tried smiling at a girl who glared at me, but she turned away real fast, and I was afraid something would happen.

During recess we tried to stay together, the four of us. We made for each other and then just stood still — until a couple of white kids came up and asked us if we wanted some milk or orange juice. We couldn't believe they had it, and we didn't know what to say anyway. So I just said "sure," trying to be as cool as I could. And I walked up and poured a glass of juice for myself like it was the kitchen at home.

At lunch I tried to act like I'd been in the place for years and knew my way around. In the afternoon I thought I might have heard a few people whispering about me when I accidentally shoved my ruler off the desk, but I didn't look around. I just picked it up and pretended to use it.

By the end of the day I was more tired than ever in my life; so tired I fell asleep on the way home. And the bus was quiet, good for sleeping.

When I got off the bus I didn't want to go right home. I wanted to think about all that had happened.

I wandered over to the old school — just to look at it. It was the same old place, only I felt sorry for it. It was real old and broken-down. It had been more fun to walk to school with Larry than to ride on the bus. I went home through the old shortcut, the alley. I missed Larry. When I got through it and passed his house I looked around. He wasn't in sight and I kept going.

Just before I got to my house I spotted him, with some older guys. He left them and came over to talk with me.

"Well, big man, how was your day?"

"It was O.K."

"O.K., O.K.," Larry said. "But what about us?" He was showing off for his big friends. "What about your brothers and sisters, all your friends over here? Do you plan to walk off, and say goodbye to us like that? Are you going to wish us nothing, and tell us 'tough luck, boys' while you rake in all they give you over there because they feel sorry for you, and want to be nice to you, so they can brag to themselves in the mirror about how good they are?"

"Look, Larry. I told you from the start I don't like leaving. But I do like what I'm getting."

"You're going to get nothing, sonny, and you'd better know it."

The guy who said that was almost as big as my father was, so I was afraid to answer him.

Larry laughed with his friends. "Tell us, boy, did they ask you to clean their shoes?" asked another boy. They were almost falling down laughing.

"No," I was too tired to say anything else.

"Explain yourself some more," Larry said, laughing right at me.

I got mad, but I tried one more time to fix things up.

"Don't think I'm kidding myself. I know those people over there. I could tell today, some of them are nice, but a lot of them only pretend to be. Even if all of them wanted to be friends with me, I'm not sure I'd do it. But that school is a good deal."

Larry shrugged his shoulders.

"Well, go ahead, Jimmy boy. We'll see. Maybe you'll be straight with yourself, or maybe you won't, and then it won't be hard for us to tell. When you come back here every day acting rich, we'll know what to do. You may find it safer to *stay* over there."

They left, and Larry went with them. I couldn't get home fast enough.

Home was questions from everyone, and my mother kissing me and telling me I looked great, and my grandma saying she'd prayed. They wanted to look at my books and I was glad to be able to tell them I had to study, so they'd leave me alone. My mother had gone and got me a table, all my own, and she put it in the hall and said it would be a room, and everyone should try to stay out and keep to the kitchen or the bedroom or go out on the street.

At supper they were all watching me and telling

me they'd be glad to do something for me if I wanted. My little brothers asked me questions and stared at me as though I'd been elected President or something, and my sister Mary kept on telling me to eat more and build up my strength. I was getting ready to scream and run downstairs to the street when my grandmother must have seen by the look on my face how I felt.

"Leave him alone, and stop waiting on him. He's had a hard day, and he needs quiet from us, not a lot of talk and those questions. Keep your words for praying."

Then I could finish my food and go rest for a few minutes. And lying down I thought of the bus. I thought of the new school and Larry back in that dead end of a school and what he said when I saw him afterwards. Then I could hear my grandma saying it was a long ride that I took and I thought to myself yes, that's right.